# Little chicken's big day

by katie davis and jerry davis

MARGARET K. McELDERRY BOOKS
New York London Toronto Sydney

special thanks to Tim Nordquist, a good egg indeed.—J. D.

special thanks to our little chickens, Ruby Davis and Benny Davis,
without whom this book wouldn't be all it's cracked up to be.
—K. D.

MARGARET K. McELDERRY BOOKS
An imprint of Simon & Schuster Children's Publishing Division
1230 Avenue of the Americas, New York, New York 10020
Text copyright © 2011 by Jerry Davis
Illustrations copyright © 2011 by Katie Davis
All rights reserved, including the right of reproduction in whole
or in part in any form.
MARGARET K. McELDERRY BOOKS is a trademark of Simon & Schuster, Inc.
For information about special discounts for bulk purchases, please
contact Simon & Schuster Special Sales at 1-866-506-1949 or
business@simonandschuster.com.
The Simon & Schuster Speakers Bureau can bring authors to your live event.
For more information or to book an event, contact the Simon & Schuster Speakers
Bureau at 1-866-248-3049 or visit our website at www.simonspeakers.com.
The text for this book is set in Chauncy DeLuxxe.
Manufactured in China
0511 SCP
10 9 8 7 6 5 4 3 2
Library of Congress Cataloging-in-Publication Data
Davis, Jerry, 1959–
Little chicken's big day / Jerry Davis and Katie Davis ; illustrated by Katie Davis.
p. cm.
Summary: Little Chicken is tired of being told what to do by Big Chicken,
but when they become separated he misses all of the clucking.
ISBN 978-1-4424-1401-3 (hc)
[1. Brothers—Fiction. 2. Chickens—Fiction.] I. Davis, Katie (Katie I.) II. Title.
PZ7.D28848Lit 2011
[E]—dc22
2010011826

To Jack and Helen Davis, the original Big Chickens.
—J. D.

To Janie Bynum, your artful insights are poultry in motion.
—K. D.

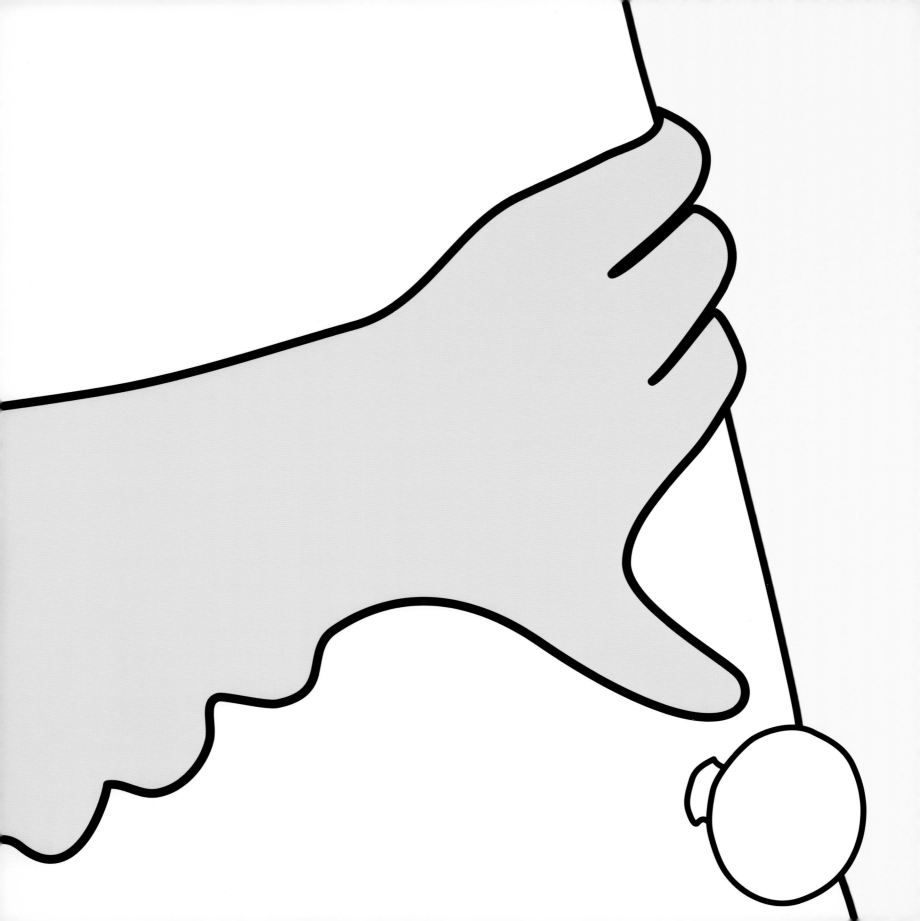

# Rise 'N' Shine!

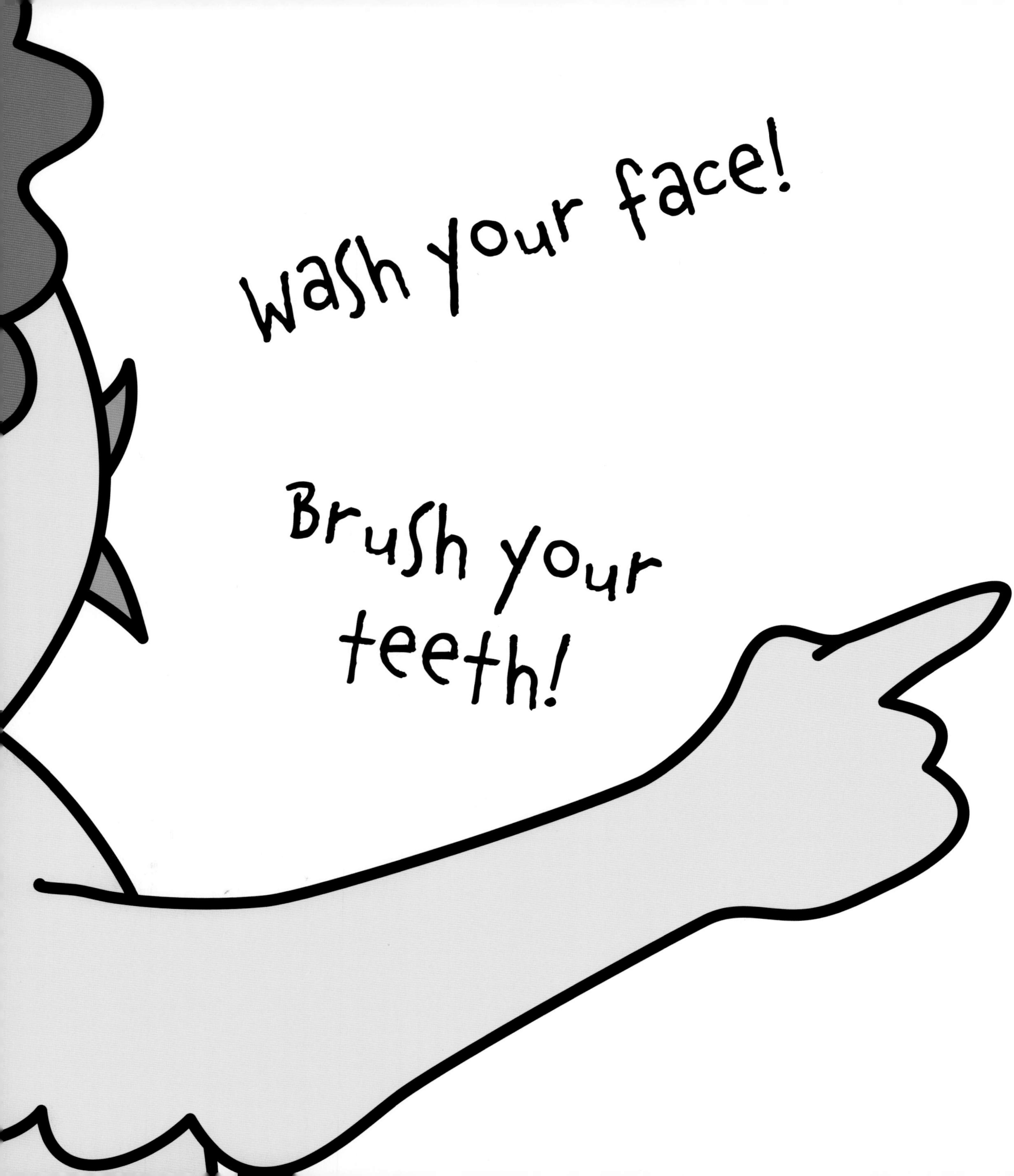

Wash your face!

Brush your teeth!

# Get dressed!

I hear you cluckin', Big chicken.

your food!

Time to go!

I hear you cluckin', big chicken.

# FOLLOW

me!

big chicken?

iicken!

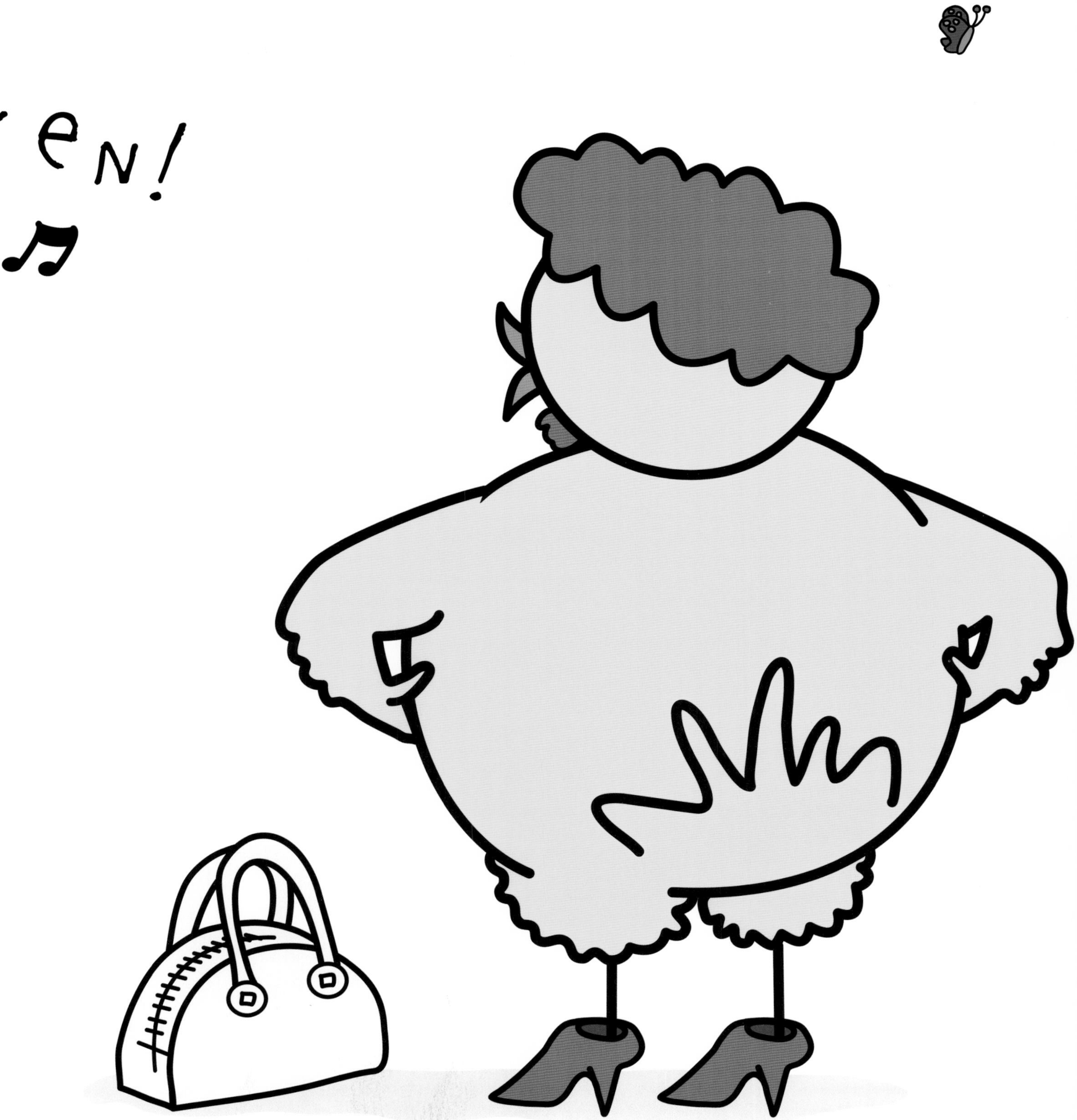

I hear you cluckin', Big chicken!

Let's go home.

story time!

sweet dreams!

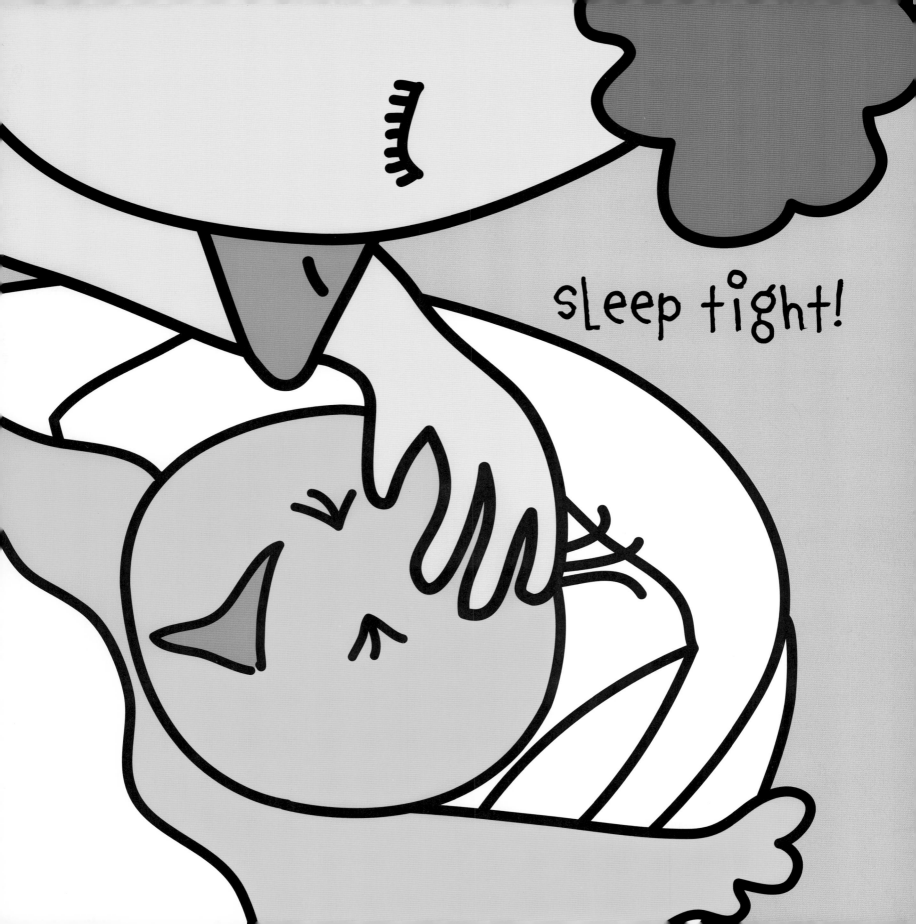

I love you, mama.

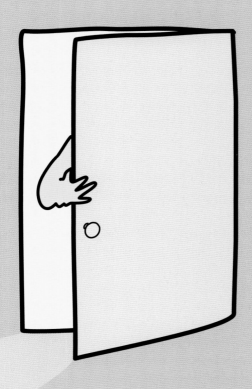

I hear you cluckin', little chicken.